For Andrea, Eric, and Lucinda
Thank you to Gail Hochman
and Anne Schwartz —U. H.

For the little people—G. P.

Atheneum Books for Young Readers
An imprint of Simon & Schuster
Children's Publishing Division
1230 Avenue of the Americas
New York, New York 10020
Text copyright © 1994 by Ursula Hegi
Text adaptation copyright © 2003 by Ursula Hegi
Illustrations copyright © 2003 by Giselle Potter
Book design by Lee Wade
The text of this book is set in Spectrum.
The illustrations are
rendered in gouache on paper.
Manufactured in China
First Edition
1 2 3 4 5 6 7 8 9 10
Library of Congress
Cataloging-in-Publication Data
Hegi, Ursula.
Trudi and Pia / by Ursula Hegi ;
illustrated by Giselle Potter.
p. cm.
"An Anne Schwartz book."
Summary: A dwarf girl goes to the circus
where she meets another dwarf
and realizes that she is not alone.
ISBN 0-689-84683-5
[1. Dwarfs—Fiction. 2. Size—Fiction.] I. Potter, Giselle,
ill. II. Title.
PZ7.H35925 Tr 2003
[E]—dc21
2001055995
The text of this book is an adaptation of
Stones from the River by Ursula Hegi.

Trudi & Pia

by
URSULA HEGI

pictures by
GISELLE POTTER

AN ANNE SCHWARTZ BOOK

Atheneum Books for Young Readers

New York   London   Toronto   Sydney   Singapore

Many nights the dwarf girl, Trudi, fell asleep hoping that her body would stretch itself overnight, that she'd wake up and be the size of other girls her age.

Sometimes, during the
day, she'd hang from
door frames or tree limbs
by her fingers until they were
numb, convinced she could feel her arms and legs getting
longer. She would tie her mother's silk scarves around her head—
one encircling her forehead, the other knotted beneath her chin—to
keep her head from growing bigger.

Aa Bb Cc Dd Ee Ff

Trudi yearned to know someone shaped like her, someone whose legs would be short, whose arms could not reach the coat hooks in her classroom, someone who would look at her with joy—not with curiosity.

But she would not meet another dwarf until she
visited the circus and saw the animal tamer lead
the elephants into the arena.

Pia was her name. Her short body moved quickly, lightly, and when her whip snapped around the elephants' massive feet, they bowed their knees for her.

While people laughed at the clowns and monkeys, they did not laugh at the dwarf woman. They were awed by her skill and courage. When she placed her head inside the lion's dangerous mouth, even the youngest children hushed, and in that long moment before she pulled out her head—that moment when the smell of animals and sawdust and sweat thickened inside the huge circus tent—one single breath connected everyone in the audience.

Pia ran into the center of the arena, sweeping one graceful arm through the air. Trudi clapped her hands until they stung, wishing that people would notice her, too, for the things she could do—like adding numbers in her head or remembering the birthday of every child in her classroom—not for being a dwarf. She wondered if Pia, too, had tried to force her body to stretch. But Pia was no taller than she.

A fat clown on a tiny bicycle wobbled into the arena, shrieking while a parrot with glorious tail feathers clung to his back like a vulture. After riding wildly around Pia, the clown threw himself into the sawdust at her feet, begging her to rescue him.

Pia snapped her fingers, and the parrot fluttered up and settled on her wrist. "I need a volunteer," she announced.

Many of the children in the audience raised their arms, but
Trudi just slid from her seat and stepped forward.

Pia looked startled. Her black eyes skipped past Trudi and back to her as if she were seeing herself in a mirror. But then she laughed with delight. "It looks like we have a volunteer. From the magic island I call home. The island of the little people, where everyone is our height—" She waved her hand from Trudi to herself. "Where figs and oranges and orchids fill every garden, where birds like Othello—" She whispered to the parrot, and it flew to Trudi's wrist. "—are as common as your ducks."

Trudi held her wrist steady. The claws of the bird were cool like the rind of an orange.

The clown squealed, grabbed his bicycle under one arm, and cartwheeled out of the ring.

"It is an island very few people know." The animal tamer fastened her gaze on Trudi. "Do you remember our island?"

Trudi's neck felt stiff as she nodded.

"And what do you remember best, my lovely friend?"

Trudi was afraid to look beyond Pia at the familiar faces in the audience. She stroked one finger across the back of the parrot. "The waterfall."

Pia nodded. "And a splendid waterfall it is. Cool in the summer, warm in the winter."

From the empty air, she whisked three golden hoops and held them up. They formed a tunnel, and the parrot screeched and flew through them, then landed back on Trudi's wrist.

"I remember a tunnel," Trudi spoke up, "made of jewels."
"It led from your house to mine, yes." In the eyes of the animal tamer was a mischievous glint that urged Trudi to go on.

Between them, they wove the story of an island so glorious that everyone in the audience would have followed them there without question, and all along the parrot flew between them like a weaver's shuttle.

Before Pia led Trudi back to her seat, she plucked a huge paper rose from the air and gave it to Trudi with a kiss.

When the tent had emptied,
Trudi went looking for Pia.

Behind the merry-go-round and the fortune teller's tent, a blue trailer sat in a patch of clover. Next to it hung a laundry line with lacy underwear and short stockings that must have been Pia's.

Trudi was afraid to knock, but she pushed
her shoulders back and raised her hand.

Pia didn't look surprised to see her.

"There must be others," Trudi blurted.

Pia stepped aside to let her enter.

"I have never met anyone like me." Trudi said it slowly.

And then she said it again. "I have never met anyone like me."

"Oh, but they're everywhere." The dwarf woman closed the door behind her. "In my travels, I never have to look for them. They find me. And just like you, they want to know about others."

"Why can't we all be in one place?" Trudi asked.

"We are," Pia told her. "It's called earth."

Trudi laid her paper rose on Pia's table. "If we lived on your island, I wouldn't be the only one then."

Pia led her to a low, stuffed chair. "You're not the only one."

"In this town I am."

When Trudi sat down, her feet touched the floor instead of dangling high above it. She smiled to herself with the promise that in this world of tall chairs, she would someday have furniture the right size for her inside her own house.

"When I get that feeling of being the only one," Pia said, "I imagine hundreds of people like me . . . all over the world, in Russia and Italy and France and Portugal, all feeling alone, and then I feel linked to them."

Trudi leaned forward. "Have you met a hundred like us?"

"I have met one hundred and four, to be exact."

"You count them?" Trudi asked.

"How can I not?"

Dizzy with joy, Trudi could feel them—those one hundred and four—linked to her as if they were here in the trailer. In that instant she understood that for Pia, being a dwarf was normal, beautiful even. To Pia, long arms were ugly, long legs unsteady. Tall people looked odd, too far from the ground.

Pia arranged apple slices on a yellow plate and handed them to Trudi. "Eat, if you like," she said.

"Thank you." Trudi chewed slowly. "Will you come back here?"

"Perhaps." Pia broke an apple slice into two pieces. Ate one piece. Then the other.

"I can't know those things ahead of time. But if you ever want to ask me questions, send them to the stars. They'll find me."

When will I see you again?

Where are you now?

Will I meet other dwarfs?

Will I ever get married?

Will I have children of my own?

Will they be short like me?

Trudi wiped her fingers on her skirt. "Do you ever wish you could look straight into people's faces?"

"Instead of always looking up and seeing the underside of their chins or the hair in their noses?" Pia giggled. "Just don't look up."

Trudi shook her head. "But then I'll only see their bellies, their elbows, their fat bottoms."

"Girl . . ." Pia dabbed tears of laughter from her eyes. "Tell me this—what do you do if someone has a very quiet voice?"

Trudi had to think for a moment. "I lean closer."

"Right." Pia said. "If you speak softly, most people will bend down to you. As long as you remember not to look up."

"I'll try that." Trudi looked around the trailer. It was smaller than her own bedroom. Still . . . she didn't need much space and could sleep on Pia's sofa. "What if I came with you?" she asked, her heartbeat high in her throat.

"But this is where you belong . . . where you matter," Pia replied.

Trudi shook her head. "I want to come with you."

    "Even if I welcomed you," Pia said, "it wouldn't change that feeling of being the only one. No one but you can change that. Like this." Pia wrapped her short arms around herself. Rocking steadily, she smiled. "Some day," she promised Trudi, "you'll remember this."